Pattacake, Pattacake, baker's man,
Bake me a cake as fast as you can;
Pat it and prick it and mark it with P,
Put it in the oven for you and for me.

Pattacake, Pattacake, baker's man,
Bake me a cake as fast as you can;
Roll it up, roll it up;
And throw it in a pan!

Pattacake, Pattacake, baker's man.

MR PATTACAKE

Stephanie Baudet

Sweet Cherry
Publishing

Published by Sweet Cherry Publishing Limited
Unit 36, Vulcan House
Vulcan Road
Leicester, LE5 3EF
United Kingdom

First published in the UK in 2017
ISBN: 978-1-78226-211-4
©Stephanie Baudet 2015
Illustrations ©Creative Books
Illustrated by Joy Das, Andy Everitt-Stewart and Joyson Loitongbam

Mr Pattacake Joins the Circus

Wai Man Book Binding (China) Ltd. Kowloon, H.K.

MR PATTACAKE
joins the
CIRCUS

'We're off to join the circus!' shouted Mr Pattacake one morning. A letter had just come through the door and he was waving it in the air dramatically. Any minute now he would break into his silly dance, which he always did when he was excited. His big chef's hat was already wobbling in anticipation.

Treacle, his ginger cat, was eating his breakfast, and hardly paused when Mr Pattacake shouted. He was used to the chef's jolly antics, and was always happy to hear about another cooking job, because it meant lots of tasty titbits for him as well.

A *circus*, though, was something different. Treacle had never been to a circus so it would be a new experience. He wasn't even sure what a circus was, but he was sure Mr Pattacake would explain it to him later on.

'I have been hired as the circus chef for a week,' said Mr Pattacake, peering through his glasses as he read. 'It's just while the circus is in town here. Their usual chef has a bad bout of sawdust allergy. Oh dear!'

'Now, I wonder...' Mr Pattacake thought out loud as he sat down at the kitchen table and reached for his pen and paper. It was time to make a list. Cooking jobs always began with him making a list, which was why he was so efficient. Good planning was very important.

'What do circus people eat?' he mused.

Treacle wondered why circus people should be any different from other people. As usual, Mr Pattacake read his mind – he always knew what Treacle was thinking, which was just as well because Treacle, of course, was a cat and couldn't talk. Not in human language, anyway.

'Circus folk live in caravans,' said Mr Pattacake. 'So there won't be a lot of space. They have very energetic jobs so they need some good food inside them.' He looked at Treacle, waiting for a response from his lazy cat.

'There'll be acrobats and jugglers,' he said. 'And clowns to make you laugh. Ponies and performing dogs…' Treacle frowned. 'And trapeze and tightrope walking.'

The only things Treacle understood from the list were the ponies and the dogs. Ponies he didn't mind – but dogs... not just any dogs, but *performing* dogs...

He wasn't sure he wanted to go anymore.

'You'll love it,' said Mr Pattacake, in an attempt to reassure Treacle. 'And it's only for a week. You don't want to stay at home on your own, do you? Or perhaps I could get Naughty Tortie to come and keep you company.'

Treacle growled and Mr Pattacake just laughed. He knew how much that mischievous tortoiseshell cat, Naughty Tortie, annoyed Treacle. In fact, he had a feeling that Treacle was actually a little afraid of her.

On the morning they were going to join the circus, Mr Pattacake went out in his little yellow van and bought all the ingredients for the meals he was planning to make for the week.

The circus was arriving little by little, with some trucks pulling caravans, and others loaded up with all sorts of circus equipment. They had begun to put up the big top on the sports field. The framework was already up and men were hauling the great canopy over the top.

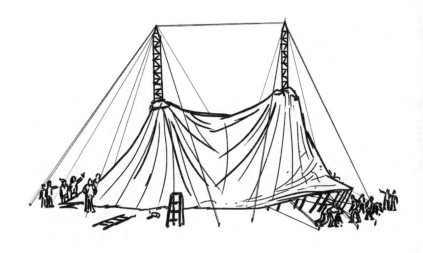

All around the field, people were busy getting ready for opening night. Some were practising their act right in front for people to see. The juggler was juggling six or seven coloured balls and a couple of acrobats were doing their warm-up exercises on the grass. They had already drawn in a small crowd of spectators and there was now quite a queue at the ticket office as well.

Mr Pattacake felt a thrill of excitement. He was going to be a part of it – even though he wouldn't actually be seen by the public. But he *would* be making sure that the performers had good meals to give them plenty of energy.

At four o'clock he and Treacle reported to the ringmaster, whose name was Mr Macaroni, an Italian man with a big moustache and a booming voice.

'Who is this?' he said, pointing at Treacle. 'We don't need any more animal acts.'

'This is my cat, Treacle,' said Mr Pattacake, defensively. 'We work together. Where I go, he goes.'

Treacle smiled to himself, proudly. *You tell him*, he thought.

'Okay,' said Mr Macaroni, nodding his head, 'but he must do something. **Everrrybody** here must work.' He rolled his *r* when he said *everybody*. '**Everrrybody** must do something,' he said again.

Mr Pattacake nodded enthusiastically, although he couldn't think of anything that Treacle could do. He did play the lute, of course, but that wasn't a circus act.

'He plays the lute,' he said, without thinking.

'The *lute*!' Mr Macaroni exclaimed, looking at Mr Pattacake in surprise. 'Why do we want a lute player in a circus?'

'Well,' said Mr Pattacake, 'a *cat* playing a lute is unusual.'

'True,' he said, agreeing. 'But no. He must do a circus act. Can he juggle?'

'Not very well,' said Mr Pattacake.

'Can he be a clown?'

'He often is,' said Mr Pattacake, chuckling.

A big smile spread over Mr Macaroni's face. 'I have it! He can do a high wire act. Cats have no fear of heights and are **verrry** sure-footed. It will be our new act.'

Treacle had listened to all this with great interest. A high wire act. He wasn't sure what that was, but he *had* seen birds sitting on the telephone wires outside their house. He'd never thought of trying it himself, though.

Perhaps this could be a new skill... Those birds would certainly get a surprise!

Mr Macaroni led them to a caravan and opened the door. It wasn't quite what Mr Pattacake had expected. There was a small, rather messy cooker and a sink on one wall. A big freezer and fridge stood on the other, plus lots of shelves, too.

There wasn't a lot of room at all.

Mr Pattacake looked round with dismay. 'What do the performers like to eat?' he asked.

'Performers?' said Mr Macaroni. 'The performers cook their own meals in their caravans. You are here to make the burgers and hot dogs and popcorn for the audiences. You will also be selling them before the show, and during the intervals.'

'Burgers?' said Mr Pattacake in disbelief. 'Hot dogs!?'

'I like to sell home-made ones,' said the ringmaster, proudly. 'No store-bought food.'

'You don't really need a chef...' began Mr Pattacake, but then he stopped. It might be fun.

Mr Macaroni turned to go, but then paused and said, 'Oh, you must also make the custard pies for the clowns to throw at each other.'

'*Real* custard pies?' asked Mr Pattacake.

'**Everrrything** must be real and home-made,' said Mr Macaroni, rolling his r again.

When the ringmaster had gone Mr Pattacake looked at the bags of food he had brought to cook the meals for the performers. Oh well, he could still take it all home and put it in his freezer for another cooking job.

Meanwhile, he thought he had better get started on the burgers and hot dogs as well as the custard pies. There was a lot to be done!

Mr Pattacake was up to his elbows in minced meat and the corn was merrily popping on the stove, when there was a knock at the door.

'Come in!' he shouted.

A small girl came in carrying a small pink sparkly costume. 'This is for your cat to wear for the high wire act,' she said, laying it down on a shelf before scurrying out again.

Treacle let out a big **yowl**, making Mr Pattacake turn quickly to see what all the fuss was about.

'What's the matter, Treacle?' He looked at the costume more closely. It was a pink tutu covered with sparkly sequins. Mr Pattacake let out a roar of laughter and his big chef's hat wobbled violently, nearly falling off with every hearty chuckle.

Treacle scowled and shook his head. No way was he going to wear a pink sparkly tutu!

Mr Pattacake took pity on him, so after washing his hands, he picked up the tutu and went out of the caravan to find Mr Macaroni.

After a bit of an argument, he arrived back at the caravan and held up the new costume.

'Is this better, Treacle?' he said, still smiling.

This time the costume was a little red cape, which didn't go too well with Treacle's ginger fur, but was certainly better than that other thing. How those performing dogs would have laughed at that! It would have been very humiliating!

When the food was ready, Mr Pattacake and Treacle went for a rehearsal. Mr Pattacake didn't need to rehearse how to sell popcorn, but Treacle *did* need to rehearse how to walk on a tightrope very high above the ground.

'Look! There's a safety net,' said Mr Pattacake, pointing it out to a very nervous-looking Treacle.

'Just one thing,' said Mr Macaroni, who had joined them. 'If you fall and land in the net, you must grab hold of it as you land, otherwise...' He swished his arm in a big arc. 'You will bounce **rrright** out again and onto the floor.'

But before even Mr Pattacake could guess what he meant, the ringmaster was already pushing Treacle towards the tightrope – that was now just above the ground.

Now Treacle was used to walking along the narrowest of fences, but fences didn't wobble like this wire rope. Fences were only a couple of metres above the ground, too, not high up like *this* rope would be tonight.

However, he did manage to wobble his way along the rope, and when he reached the end, Mr Macaroni waved his hands in the air as he walked away. 'You'll be okay, **Trrreacle**.'

All too soon it was time for the show. Excited children, along with their parents, poured into the big top and took their seats, chattering happily in anticipation.

Mr Pattacake put on his big chef's hat and went out amongst the audience to sell popcorn from his tray. He had made some really interesting flavours, like gingerbread, peanut butter, crispy bacon and maple syrup. There was also strawberry cheesecake and even caramel flavour.

Meanwhile, Treacle was in the dressing room at the side of the big top putting on his sparkly red cape.

His ears were flattened and his tail down as he imagined walking across that tightrope high in the air...

The band struck up, there was a drum roll, and Mr Macaroni walked out into the ring, cracking his whip.

The show had begun.

Mr Pattacake hurried away to prepare the hot dogs and burgers. He didn't want to miss Treacle's act.

First came the acrobats and then the clown, making everyone laugh with his antics. The audience was settling down to a fun evening, their laughter echoing through the big top.

After that, the ponies cantered in with poodles on their backs and girls dancing around them. Round and round the ring they went, with the poodles doing all sorts of tricks, making the audience applaud and cheer.

At last it was Treacle's turn.

'Ladies and gentlemen! Boys and girls!' shouted
Mr Macaroni in his booming ringmaster's voice.
'For the first time in this circus, I present to you,
the very talented high wire walker, **Trrreacle**!'

There was thunderous applause as Treacle ran
in and headed for the ladder. Slowly, he climbed

up to the tightrope. Up and up. Higher and higher.
He daren't look down.

He reached the little platform.

Usually, high wire walkers carried a long pole to help them balance, but Treacle was a cat and couldn't do that. He only had his four paws.

There was a drumroll and he slowly stepped out onto the wire.

The audience hushed, all eyes looking up at the small ginger cat, making his way slowly along the wire, his little red sparkly cape reflecting the big, bright lights.

When he got to the middle, he made a mistake. He looked down.

Then he **WOBBLED**.

And you know that once a wobble starts, it's hard to stop it. It **WOBBLED** him right off the wire. A great gasp went up from the audience as they watched Treacle fall.

Down and down he fell, right into the safety net.

What had Mr Macaroni said? If you fall into the net, you must grab hold of it.

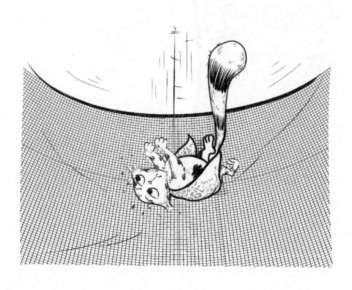

Now, it's quite difficult for a cat to grab hold of anything. They have claws, but no *real* fingers.

Treacle landed in the net and just bounced right out again, landing in the ring next to a very worried looking Mr Macaroni.

But, being a cat, he landed perfectly on his feet. The audience roared in amazement, thinking that it was all part of the act.

Mr Pattacake had watched all this with his heart in his mouth. Now, as Treacle bowed his head and walked away proudly, he sighed with relief.

It was time for him to set up his burger stall for the interval.

The rest of the performance went well, and when Treacle and the other performers went on for their final bow, Treacle got a great cheer. Mr Macaroni was very pleased and said that the cat should keep the fall as part of the performance every time.

The next day, when Mr Pattacake was selling popcorn before the show, the clown, Chuckles, was doing his warm-up act in the ring. Suddenly, a bag of flour landed on Mr Pattacake's head and burst open, knocking off his big chef's hat and sending puffy clouds of white flour all over Mr Pattacake's startled face.

He dropped the tray of popcorn, which scattered all over the people sitting nearby.

The audience shrieked with laughter, causing those just taking their seats to turn to see what was happening. The people who were nearby dived to pick up the popcorn.

Mr Pattacake was certainly surprised and a little embarrassed at being part of the show, at the butt of the clown's joke, but he smiled just the same.

The next day, as he walked across the edge of the ring, Chuckles, the clown, squirted Mr Pattacake with orange-coloured water from a water pistol. At least the flour had been white to match his big chef's hat and his big white apron, but this time he was drenched in orange!

His big chef's hat had splodges of orange on it and drooped down on one side, and his nice clean white apron dripped orange liquid onto the sawdust of the ring.

Again, the audience roared and Mr Pattacake just smiled.

Each day the clown played a trick on Mr Pattacake, and he was getting a bit fed up with it. It was really spoiling his week with the circus. A joke is a joke, but it's not funny if it's repeated too often. Of course, as there was a different audience each night, it was always new to them.

Mr Pattacake did not want to be a spoilsport, but as the final night arrived, he got so annoyed that he decided that Chuckles should have a taste of his own medicine.

He got to work in the kitchen while Treacle lay on the only chair in the caravan, resting before his performance. He, too, had had his week at the circus spoilt by the performing poodles, who were jealous of his popularity and had constantly teased him.

One particular poodle, called Fifi, had very much reminded Treacle of that mischievous tortoiseshell cat, Naughty Tortie. It was a wonder she herself hadn't come to see what the circus was all about.

The final performance was in the afternoon because it was Saturday. After that, the circus folk would pack up their things and move to the next town, ready to reopen on Monday night.

As usual, Chuckles, the clown, played a *not-so-funny* trick on Mr Pattacake. This time, as Mr Pattacake walked towards the audience with his tray of popcorn, Chuckles suddenly sprang out from behind a curtain, squeezing a klaxon.

The noise was so loud and hideous that Mr Pattacake jumped in the air, scattering his tray of popcorn all over the ground. Not only that, but he shrieked with fright.

The audience roared with laughter.

Mr Pattacake had been expecting *something*, so this time he had made sure that the bags of popcorn were well closed. All he had to do was to pick them up and put them back on the tray.

The clown's trick hadn't bothered him one bit. This was their last night, and Chuckles was in for a surprise!

Mr Macaroni had lost his whip, so he was not in a good mood. Now, circuses no longer have lions and elephants to crack whips at, but they still made a great sound, so ringmasters still liked to have one. To go out into the ring without one just didn't seem right.

Just before Mr Macaroni made his entrance, whilst complaining about the lost whip, Mr Pattacake had one of his great ideas. He ran back to the caravan where he did the cooking and came back holding some long strands of spaghetti.

'I tried to make you some pasta,' he said. 'But it was much too tough. I hadn't thrown it away because I don't like waste, but maybe it will make a good whip.'

Mr Macaroni took hold of the spaghetti and gave it a sharp flick.

CRACK!

The half-cooked spaghetti was even better than his whip! He marched into the ring confidently, cracking the spaghetti strands. No one would ever know.

Treacle did his final high wire act and the applause was so great that the ringmaster offered him a permanent job.

But although Treacle, too, had enjoyed his experience in the circus, he thought he would be glad to get home to more normal jobs.

Later on in the show the clowns came on: Chuckles and his side-kick, Little Bob.

During the routine, Little Bob *always* threw a custard pie at Chuckles – full in the face.

Splat!

And it was Mr Pattacake who made the custard pies. Real ones, just as Mr Macaroni liked.

Mr Pattacake handed them the pies as usual. This time though, he had made his *real* custard pies a little differently. These ones had a surprising extra ingredient.

Little Bob picked up the custard pie, aimed, and threw it right in Chuckles' face.

Splat!

A terrible **smell** billowed out from the splattered pie. Both clowns, especially Chuckles, ran out of the ring, holding their noses – and that wasn't easy because they had red plastic noses over their real ones.

Mr Pattacake had put a stink bomb into the custard pie!

The trouble was though, that the stink began to spread throughout the big tent – and now the audience was groaning and holding their noses. Many had stood up and were trying to get outside as fast as they could.

Mr Macaroni was running about frantically, trying to get everyone to calm down and stay.

What bad publicity this would be. Who was responsible?

Mr Pattacake hadn't realised what a panic it would cause. All he had thought about was getting his revenge on Chuckles. Oh dear! What could he do?

He ran outside and shouted out to everyone, 'Stop! Don't go! The show isn't finished!'

Then he began to do his silly dance right there in the middle of the field, his big chef's hat bobbing up and down too. Treacle came running out with his lute and began to play in an attempt to get everyone to stay.

The people hesitated, and then turned round. Soon, they began to sit down on the grass, laughing at Mr Pattacake's cavorting and marvelling at a cat playing a lute.

Some of the children got up and danced too.

Mr Macaroni had stopped panicking and a smile had now spread across his face. All was not lost. Mr Pattacake had come to the rescue once again, although he suspected that it was he who had caused the panic in the first place.

Some of the acrobats came out and began their acts, along with the jugglers. The horses and the performing poodles did their routine outside too. Even the high wire walkers rigged up a wire – although it wasn't as high as the one in the tent. The people still had a wonderful view though. The only performers who couldn't do their part of the show outside were the trapeze artists.

Other people besides the audience gathered at the edge of the field to watch, and a reporter took pictures.

Mr Macaroni smiled. This was great publicity and would sell lots of tickets for their next town, which was only a few miles away.

Finally, Chuckles the clown, and Little Bob, came out to entertain the crowd again. Chuckles had forgiven Mr Pattacake for the stink bomb custard pie. After all, he had really deserved something like that after tricking Mr Pattacake all week.

They shook hands – and there was a very rude noise! But Mr Pattacake gave a genuine smile this time. Clowns couldn't help being clowns, and had to take the opportunity of playing tricks on people whenever they could. He laughed along with the audience.

When the show finished and the circus folk began to pack up, Mr Pattacake and Treacle said goodbye to them all, and promised to see them next year when they came again.

They finally arrived home to find Naughty Tortie on the doorstep. She had a big frown on her face.

'Oh dear, Naughty Tortie,' said Mr Pattacake, apologetically. 'We forgot to tell you about the circus – and we had such fun, too.'

But Treacle smiled his cat's smile. He hadn't forgotten to tell her. Who knew what kind of mischief would have happened if *she* had been there too?